Disney's
SPORT GOOFY
AND THE RACING ROBOT

A GOLDEN BOOK • NEW YORK
Western Publishing Company, Inc., Racine, Wisconsin 53404

The crowd was on their feet and cheering! The news
photographers were snapping pictures! With a late
burst of speed, Sport Goofy had won the race!

"What a great athlete Sport Goofy is!" shouted a fan.

"He runs like the wind!" exclaimed another.

But there was one spectator who hadn't come to cheer for Sport Goofy to win. His name was Big Bad Pete—and he was a crook.

Pete watched while the mayor awarded Sport
Goofy a trophy. Then the mayor handed Sport Goofy a
check for a great deal of money.

"That's the last prize money Sport Goofy is going to
win," Pete muttered to himself. "Next time, I'll be the
one who will collect the check!" With that, Pete
stomped away.

The mayor wanted to make a long speech, but Sport Goofy quickly excused himself.

"I have some errands to run," said Sport Goofy, and he went on his way.

First Sport Goofy ran to the bank and cashed his check. Next he dashed into a store where he bought racquets and bats and balls. After that, he raced all the way across town.

He stopped running when he arrived at the orphanage.

"Look what I have for you," he said to the boys and girls.

The children's eyes always brightened with joy when Sport Goofy came to visit them. He was their best friend.

Each and every child thanked Sport Goofy for the equipment. The director of the orphanage also thanked him.

"There's another race next week," Sport Goofy told them. "If I win the prize money again, I'm going to buy that field over there for you children. Then you'll have lots of room to run and play!"

In the meantime, Big Bad Pete was planning something very dishonest. He was putting together a robot. When it was completed, Pete was going to enter it in the race against Sport Goofy.

"My robot will look so much like a real person," snarled Pete to himself, "it will fool everybody!"

A week later, the runners arrived at the track. Once again, crowds of people came to watch Sport Goofy run. Everyone was glad to see Sport Goofy. They didn't pay any attention to the new runner that Pete had entered.

"His name is Zippy," Pete told the entry judge.

While the runners were lining up to begin the race, Pete hid behind a nearby fence. He wanted to be sure no one saw him pressing the buttons on the control unit that would make his robot run.

The starter gave the signal and–*WHOOSH!*–the athletes were off and running. Sport Goofy had a determined look on his face. He was thinking of the children in the orphanage. "I have to win this race so I can buy that playing field for them," he thought.

Looking out from his hiding place, Pete began to worry. Sport Goofy was running farther ahead of Zippy the Robot with every step.

Before long, the runners were nearing the finish line. "No you don't, Sport Goofy!" growled Pete. He pressed the "EXTRA FAST" button on his control unit and–*ZOOM!*–Zippy streaked ahead and won the race.

Sport Goofy felt sad. Losing the race meant he would not be able to buy the playing field for his friends. Still, he congratulated the winner, for he was always a good sport.

The mayor also shook hands with Zippy and said, "Here's your trophy. And here's your check."

At that very instant, Pete appeared and rudely
snatched the check from the mayor's hand.

"I'll take that," he growled. "I'm his manager!" There
was a reason for Pete to hurry. He had made his flimsy
robot run EXTRA FAST, and now he was afraid it
would begin falling apart.

Grabbing hold of Zippy's hand, Pete started to run.

Suddenly, puffs of smoke came out of the robot's ears.

A spring inside the robot snapped, and—*PING!*—its head flew off! Everybody gasped in surprise.

"That isn't a PERSON," said the mayor. "It's a ROBOT!"

As more pieces of Zippy began dropping, Pete let go of the robot and tried to flee with the trophy and check.

The mayor stepped in front of him. "Oh, no, you don't, you scoundrel!" he said.

"Robots don't belong in races with PEOPLE," said the mayor. "That's cheating."

The mayor took the trophy and check from Big Bad Pete and gave them to Sport Goofy. "You are the rightful winner," he declared.

"Whenever I cheat I get caught!" Pete grumbled.

The day after the race, Sport Goofy kept his promise. He bought the playing field with his prize money.

"The boys and girls will get a lot of good exercise now," said Sport Goofy to the director of the orphanage.

The director nodded his head in agreement.
"You are truly the best friend a child could ever
have, Sport Goofy!" he said.